LYRICS BY MIKE CRAVER

# Beaver Ball at

Tonight!

PICTURES BY JOAN KAGHAN

# the Bug Club

MUSIC BY MARK HARDWICK / DEBRA MONK

FARRAR, STRAUS AND GIROUX

NEW YORK

Beaver Ball at the Bug Club
The sign said "Eight"

Squirrels were lining up for blocks

Bunnies in their Easter frocks

Drinking bug juice on the rocks
In Ole Back Bay

Old Miss Goose is acting queer
Ain't laid eggs since last year
Fussin' and a-fumin'
Tossin' and a-turnin'
Hissin' and a-moanin'
Those barnyard blues
Beaver Ball at the Bug Club down by Ole Back Bay

Old Man Muskrat's lookin' pallid
Fill him up on 'tater salad
Pluck his twanger

Slap his jaw

Send him down to Beaver Hall

The night was dark, the sky was blue
Around the dam the beavers flew

Cleanin', preenin',

gnawin', sawin',

humpin', thumpin' that old dam in two

Shooey! You never saw a solemn eye, an empty paw
Beaver Ball at the Bug Club down by Ole Back Bay

So puff your muff,

brush your tail

Pack your sack,

bring some snails

Beaver Ball at the Bug Club

Beaver Ball at the Bug Club

Beaver Ball at the Bug Club
down by Ole Back Bay

# Beaver Ball at the Bug Club

Lyrics by Mike Craver    Music by Mark Hardwick and Debra Monk

*For Bob and Alexander*

Library of Congress catalog card number: 89-46481
Published simultaneously in Canada by HarperCollins*Canada Ltd*
Printed and bound in the United States of America
Designed by Martha Rago
First edition, 1992